To

PEACHTREE

With love from

THE
Twelve Days
OF Christmas

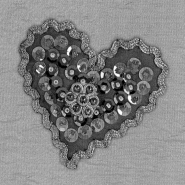

For my fantastic sisters,
Kiwi and Biddy
— *R. G.*

Barefoot Books
2067 Massachusetts Ave
Cambridge, MA 02140

Barefoot Books
294 Banbury Road
Oxford, OX2 7ED

First published in Great Britain by Barefoot Books, Ltd
and in the United States of America by Barefoot Books, Inc in 2002
This expanded hardback edition first published in 2015

Graphic design by Barefoot Books
Reproduction by Bright Arts, Singapore
Printed in China on 100% acid-free paper
This book was typeset in Anne Bonny and Arrus BT
The illustrations were created with embroidered collage and handmade papers

ISBN 978-1-78285-221-6

British Cataloguing-in-Publication Data:
a catalogue record for this book is available from the British Library

Library of Congress Cataloging-in-Publication Data
is available under LCCN 2008271195

1 3 5 7 9 8 6 4 2

THE
Twelve Days
OF Christmas

Rachel Griffin

PEACHTREE

Barefoot Books
step inside a story

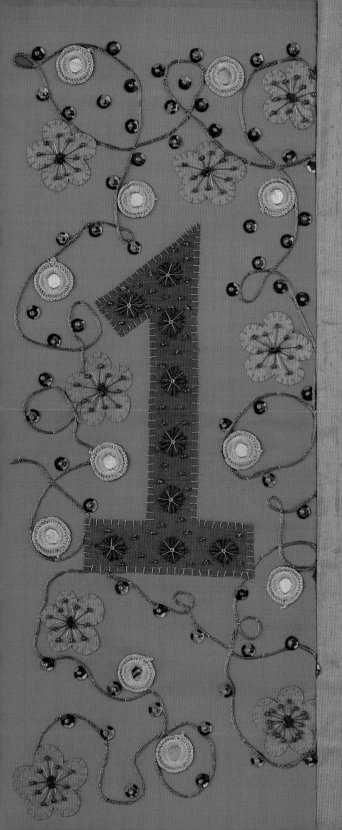

On the **first** day of Christmas
My true love gave to me

A partridge in a pear tree.

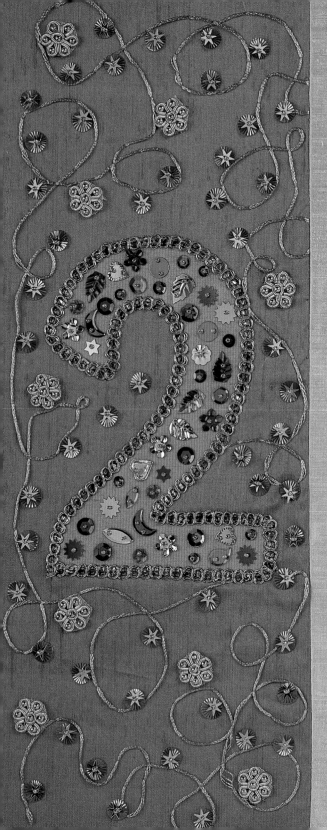

On the **second** day of Christmas
My true love gave to me

Two turtle doves
And a partridge in a pear tree.

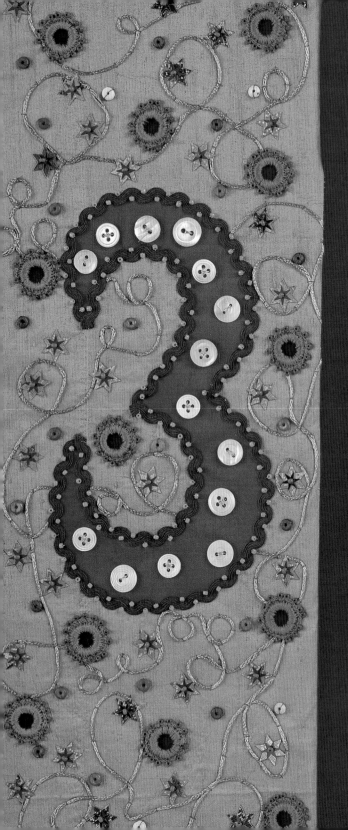

On the **third** day of Christmas
My true love gave to me

Three French hens,
Two turtle doves
And a partridge in a pear tree.

On the **fourth** day of Christmas
My true love gave to me

Four calling birds,
Three French hens,
Two turtle doves
And a partridge in a pear tree.

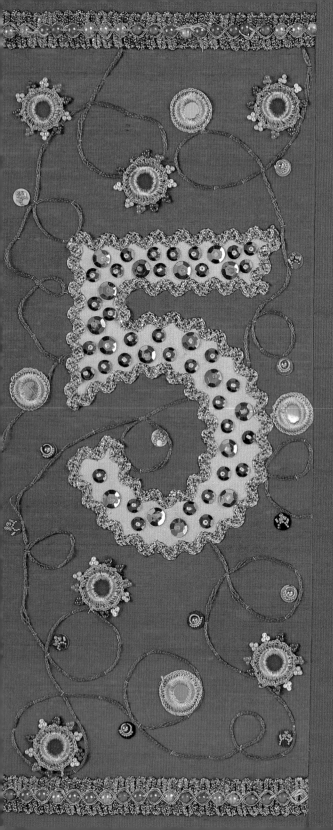

On the **fifth** day of Christmas
My true love gave to me

Five golden rings,
Four calling birds,
Three French hens,
Two turtle doves
And a partridge in a pear tree.

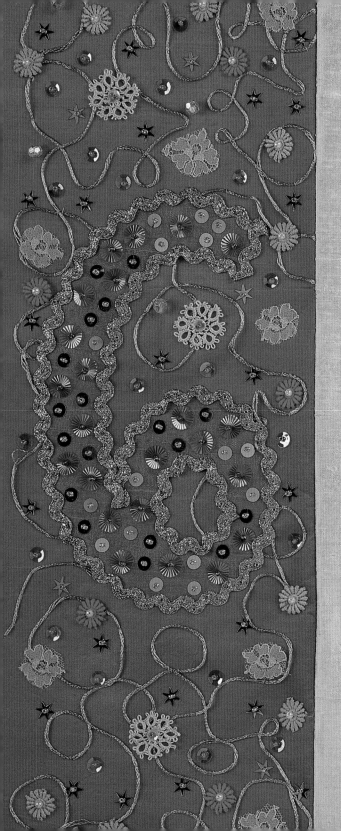

On the **sixth** day of Christmas
My true love gave to me

Six geese a-laying,
Five golden rings,
Four calling birds,
Three French hens,
Two turtle doves
And a partridge in a pear tree.

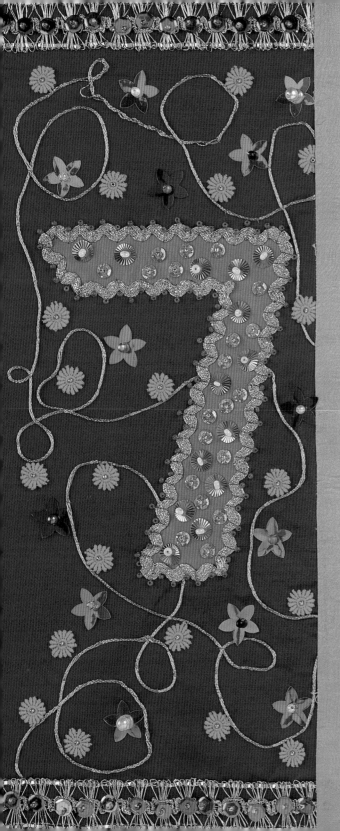

On the **seventh** day of Christmas
My true love gave to me

Seven swans a-swimming,
Six geese a-laying,
Five golden rings,
Four calling birds,
Three French hens,
Two turtle doves
And a partridge in a pear tree.

On the **eighth** day of Christmas
My true love gave to me

Eight maids a-milking,
Seven swans a-swimming,
Six geese a-laying,
Five golden rings,
Four calling birds,
Three French hens,
Two turtle doves
And a partridge in a pear tree.

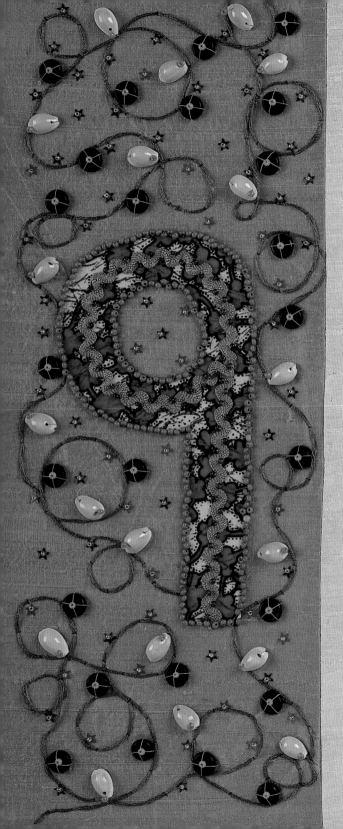

On the **ninth** day of Christmas
My true love gave to me

Nine drummers drumming,
Eight maids a-milking,
Seven swans a-swimming,
Six geese a-laying,
Five golden rings,
Four calling birds,
Three French hens,
Two turtle doves
And a partridge in a pear tree.

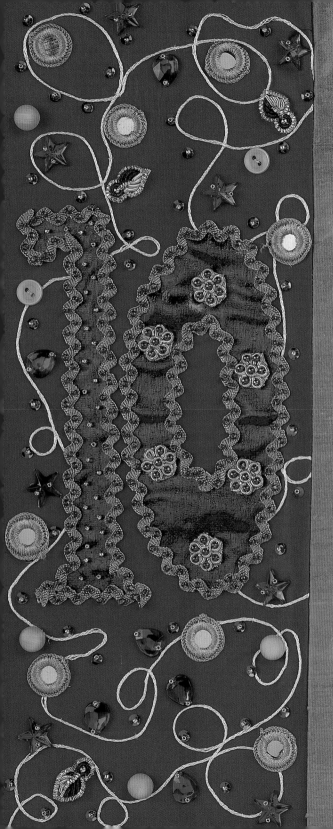

On the **tenth** day of Christmas
My true love gave to me

Ten pipers piping,
Nine drummers drumming,
Eight maids a-milking,
Seven swans a-swimming,
Six geese a-laying,
Five golden rings,
Four calling birds,
Three French hens,
Two turtle doves
And a partridge in a pear tree.

On the **eleventh** day of Christmas
My true love gave to me

Eleven ladies dancing,
Ten pipers piping,
Nine drummers drumming,
Eight maids a-milking,
Seven swans a-swimming,
Six geese a-laying,
Five golden rings,
Four calling birds,
Three French hens,
Two turtle doves
And a partridge in a pear tree.

On the **twelfth** day of Christmas
My true love gave to me

Twelve lords a-leaping,
Eleven ladies dancing,
Ten pipers piping,
Nine drummers drumming,
Eight maids a-milking,
Seven swans a-swimming,
Six geese a-laying,
Five golden rings,
Four calling birds,
Three French hens,
Two turtle doves
And a partridge in a pear tree.

Twelve Days of Christmas

The Twelve Days of Christmas is a Christian festive season that celebrates the birth of Jesus Christ. In most places, it is celebrated from 25 December (Christmas Day) until 5 January. However, the festival has ancient origins that predate the birth of Jesus. Many pre-Christian societies brightened the dark days following the winter solstice (21 December) with songs, drinking games, music making, storytelling and other festivities. It was a natural time of year to make merry: meat was plentiful after the autumn slaughtering season, fruits had fermented into wine and there was not much work to be done on the land. This ancient spirit of revelry is preserved in the celebration of the Twelve Days of Christmas.

Twelfth Night

The last night of the Twelve Days of Christmas is celebrated with a festival called Twelfth Night. The tradition dates back to pre-Christian celebrations like Yuletide (Celtic and Gaelic) and Saturnalia (Roman). At Saturnalia, the social order was turned upside down — kings became commoners and vice versa. The celebration of Twelfth Night is the setting and subject of Shakespeare's play *Twelfth Night, or What You Will*.

The Epiphany

The Twelve Days of Christmas concludes with the feast of the Epiphany, which is usually celebrated on 6 January. In Western Christianity, the Epiphany commemorates the visit of the three wise men to the Christ child. In Eastern Christianity, it commemorates Jesus's baptism in the River Jordan. In some countries, the Epiphany marks the beginning of Carnival season, which concludes with the celebration of Mardi Gras.

Traditions

Food

In many countries, the end of the Twelve Days of Christmas is observed with the baking of a special cake for the feast of the Epiphany called a king cake or Twelfth Night cake. This cake often has a toy or dried bean baked into it that represents the baby Jesus. Depending upon where you are, the person who finds the toy or bean might be made king or queen for the day — or they might be made responsible for making the next cake or throwing the next party! In some countries, the cake also contains a clove, which represents a villain, and a twig, which represents a fool.

Gifts

Some people observe the twelve days by giving a gift on each day. Each gift represents a wish for the corresponding month of the new year.

Decoration

Christmas wreaths are traditionally crafted out of greenery and fruits on Christmas Eve, and hung on the door from Christmas Night until Twelfth Night. In many countries, it is still considered bad luck to leave Christmas decorations hanging past the morning of the Epiphany. The traditional making of wreaths probably originated in pre-Christian Europe. During the Celtic celebration of Yuletide, houses were decorated with evergreens to represent strength and the circle of life.

Yule Log

Many cultures celebrate the Twelve Days of Christmas with the lighting of the Yule log, which is a special log lit on Christmas Eve and kept burning throughout the twelve days. It is customary to light the Yule log from the saved end of the previous year's log.

History of the Song

The song "The Twelve Days of Christmas" follows a cumulative structure, which means that new lyrics are added to each verse, so that each verse is longer than the one before. Like the holiday itself, the song has ancient roots, extending far back into the oral tradition. One of the earliest print versions dates back to a 13th-century manuscript in the library of Trinity College at Cambridge University. The best-known English version was printed in 1780 in a children's book called *Mirth without Mischief*.

The Game

"The Twelve Days of Christmas" may have originated as a sort of memory game for children. The leader would recite a verse, and each player would repeat the verse from memory. Then the leader would add another verse, and then another, until one of the players made a mistake. Whoever made a mistake would have to pay a "forfeit" like a treat or a kiss.

Number of Gifts

According to the lyrics, a grand total of 364 gifts have been delivered by the 12th day of Christmas — only one short of the 365 days needed to complete the old year and start the new one. The final gift, which ensures that life flows on, is the gift of true love.

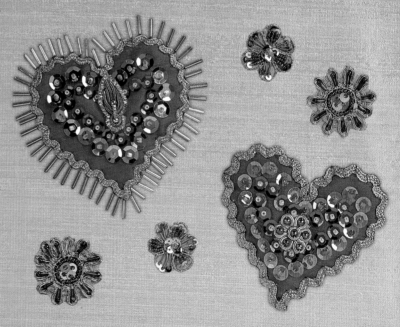

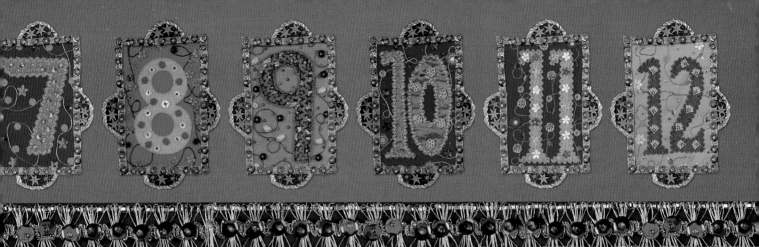

Meanings of the Gifts

There is a theory that "The Twelve Days of Christmas" was used to teach Catholic doctrine to children in England during periods of religious suppression. According to this theory, the gifts have the following meaning:

One **partridge:** Jesus Christ

Two **turtle doves:** the Old and New Testaments

Three **French hens:** the Christian virtues of faith, hope and charity

Four **calling birds:** Matthew, Mark, Luke and John, the gospel writers

Five **golden rings:** the first five books of the Old Testament (also known as the Torah or Pentateuch)

Six **geese:** the days of creation

Seven **swans:** the gifts of the Holy Spirit

Eight **maids:** the Beatitudes

Nine **drummers:** the fruits of the Holy Spirit

Ten **pipers:** the Commandments

Eleven **ladies:** the faithful apostles

Twelve **lords:** the points of doctrine in the Apostles' Creed

Illustrator's Note

When I was invited to illustrate *The Twelve Days of Christmas*, I thought back to the many versions of the book I had seen as a child, all of which were rather old-fashioned and traditionally English in character. So I decided to take a different approach and try using images from around the world. Why not have pipers from India and drummers from Malawi?

I took my inspiration from my travels. I have spent time in several European and African countries, as well as in Mexico, Australia and New Zealand. I always take my sketchbook when I am overseas, and I love to seek out quirky art galleries and museums, finding inspiration in the local designs. When I started each new piece for this book, I chose one colour that reminded me of the country I wanted to evoke, and then worked out the rest of the palette. My favourite illustration is the three French hens. I was living in France for three months while I was working on this project, so the piece brings back happy memories of the hens that roamed in the garden there, laying eggs in the flower beds.

I have been collecting since I was 12 years old. My studio is lined with jars and jars of beads, buttons, threads, laces, stamps and other treasures I use to create my hand-sewn collages. I'm always looking for new pieces to add to my collection, whether I'm abroad or sifting through jumble sales and antique markets back home. I never buy online, because finding the treasures myself is part of my creative process. Putting together the different pieces for *The Twelve Days of Christmas* brought back all kinds of memories for me — not only of my childhood Christmases but also of the different parts of the world I have explored. I hope you enjoy the result!

Barefoot Books
step inside a story

At Barefoot Books, we celebrate art and story that opens the hearts and minds of children from all walks of life, focusing on themes that encourage independence of spirit, enthusiasm for learning and respect for the world's diversity. The welfare of our children is dependent on the welfare of the planet, so we source paper from sustainably managed forests and constantly strive to reduce our environmental impact. Playful, beautiful and created to last a lifetime, our products combine the best of the present with the best of the past to educate our children as the caretakers of tomorrow.

www.barefootbooks.com